Peter Goes

Follow Finn

A search-and-find maze book

GECKO PRESS

Finn wakes up with a start. What a racket! The goblins are on the loose and everything's in chaos. Big Goblin and his rascally gang race outside. Finn's dog Sep heads off in pursuit. Quickly, Finn hunts for his clothes—they're all over the place!—so he can join the chase.

In the darkness, Finn tries to find his way.
The winding path is lit here and there by mysterious eyes. Finn hears barking,
but by the time he tracks Sep down, the goblins have disappeared again.

Finn and Sep arrive in a garden with a tangle of plants and hedges. A great castle looms in the distance. Finn catches a glimpse of Big Goblin slipping into a dark cave. Finn searches for a lamp to light the way through the green labyrinth.

The goblins' trail winds deep underground. Wriggling creatures flee from the circle of lamplight. Finn and Sep get lost in the gloomy caves. Luckily, they find a drooling rock, a royal rat and an old dragon pointing the way through the castle dungeons.

The castle is a confusion of stairways, halls and bridges.
Most of the castle creatures are asleep and all the doors are locked.
Carefully, Finn and Sep look for the key to match each lock.

In the crisscross of towers and battlements, two dogs, three bulls, five rabbits, seven cats and eleven guards lead Finn and Sep astray. A flying carpet comes to the rescue. "There goes Big Goblin!" Finn shouts. "After him!"

Finn and Sep continue their wild pursuit through a swarm of dragons, thunderclouds and flashes of lightning. Rain soaks the flying carpet. They fall from the sky into the stormy sea.

*S*hip ahoy! Finn and Sep splash down near an old ship. A compass on the spooky wreck guides them in the right direction. They brave the wild waves in search of land.

An enormous wave! The rowboat capsizes, plunging Finn and Sep into a strange underwater world. They swim between the coral reefs and anemones and come across nine helpful starfish along the way.

Finn and Sep collide with a wall of rock and realize they have reached land. They clamber up, past teetering stones, countless rabbits, love-struck mountain goats and an awful lot of bird poop.

Finn and Sep have wandered for days through the dense forest. They've lost the trail, but seven owls point the way. Sep suddenly starts to bark excitedly. He smells the scents of home. Yes! There's the house between the trees.

Big Goblin has invited everyone to a
...and presents of course!

Did you find in each picture the two little soldiers,
a present, the platypus pair and all the goblins?

First American edition published 2018 by Gecko Press USA,
an imprint of Gecko Press Ltd.

This edition first published in 2017 by Gecko Press
PO Box 9335, Wellington 6141, New Zealand
info@geckopress.com

English-language edition © Gecko Press Ltd 2017
Translation © Bill Nagelkerke 2017

© 2017, Lannoo Publishers
Original title: *Feest voor Finn*. Translated from the Dutch language.
lannoo.com

petergoes.com
facebook.com/petergoesillustrator
instagram.com/goes.peter

Distributed in the United States and Canada by Lerner Publishing Group,
lernerbooks.com
Distributed in the United Kingdom by Bounce Sales and Marketing,
bouncemarketing.co.uk
Distributed in Australia by Scholastic Australia,
scholastic.com.au
Distributed in New Zealand by Upstart Distribution,
upstartpress.co.nz

The translation of this book was funded by the Flemish Literature Fund
flemishliterature.be

Flemish
Literature
Fund

Edited by Penelope Todd
Typesetting by Vida & Luke Kelly
Printed in Belgium

For more curiously good books, visit geckopress.com